# SHIRLEY
# & JAMILA

## save their summer

by Gillian Goerz

 Dial Books for Young Readers

TO THE FRIENDSHIPS THAT CHANGED
ME FOR THE BETTER
—G.G.

Dial Books for Young Readers
An imprint of Penguin Random House LLC, New York

Copyright © 2020 by Gillian Goerz

Visit us online at penguinrandomhouse.com

Library of Congress Cataloging-in-Publication Data is available.

Hardcover ISBN 9780525552857

1 3 5 7 9 10 8 6 4 2

Paperback ISBN 9780525552864

1 3 5 7 9 10 8 6 4 2

Manufactured in China
Design by Jennifer Kelly and Gillian Goerz
Text set in GG Sans with permission of the author

Produced with the support of the City of Toronto through the
Toronto Arts Council and the Ontario Arts Council

# Chapter 1

A GARAGE SALE. THAT'S WHAT STARTED EVERYTHING.

JAMILA.

THAT'S ME.

CARRY YOUR BALL NOW PLEASE.

THAT'S MY MOM.

"SAY-HAR"?

"**SAH**-HUR."

OKAY... WELCOME TO THE NEIGHBORHOOD.

YOUR GIRL'S WHAT? NINE?

SHE JUST TURNED TEN RECENTLY. I HAD HOPED THERE WOULD BE MORE CHILDREN HER AGE IN THE NEIGHBORHOOD.

THAT'S FUNNY...

OH?

YOU'RE THE SECOND PERSON TODAY THAT'S SAID THAT TO ME!

ANOTHER MOTHER—NOW WHERE IS SHE?—JUST SAID SHE WISHED HER TEN-YEAR-OLD HAD A LOCAL GIRL TO PLAY WITH.

REALLY? I'M SURE JAMILA WOULD LOVE TO MEET—

YES! WELL... THERE'S A CHANCE YOUR GIRL WON'T CARE FOR HER.

4

OH, I'M SORRY. WERE YOU LOOKING AT THI—

NO—I WAS JUST ... UH ...

OH! LOOKIE HERE! HAVE YOU TWO MET ALREADY?

SHIRLEY, THIS IS JAIME! YOU ARE BOTH TEN YEARS OLD AND SHE—

SHE ONLY HAS OLDER BROTHERS.

YOU THOUGHT SINCE WE'RE BOTH GOING INTO GRADE FIVE, WE COULD BE FRIENDS.

OH, YOU LITTLE SHOW OFF! I'LL LEAVE YOU TWO TO GET ACQUAINTED.

5

DO YOU HATE DANCE? **I'D** HATE DANCE, BUT YOU...

HM, YES, I SEE.

DANCE IS FINE. I JUST HAVE **OTHER OCCUPATIONS** THAT REQUIRE MY ABSOLUTE FOCUS... AND LESS ADULT SUPERVISION.

WHAT "OTHER OCCU—"

IT'S OUTRAGEOUS!

TEN YEARS OLD IS CERTAINLY OLD ENOUGH TO GO OUT ALONE IN DAYLIGHT IN OUR OWN NEIGHBORHOOD!

MAYBE IF...

YOU'RE QUITE RIGHT.

I SUSPECT OUR MOMS CAN BE MADE TO AGREE. THEY WANT US TO FIND FRIENDS.

HOW DID...?

WE SPEND THE SUMMER TOGETHER. I'LL GO WITH YOU TO THE BASKETBALL COURT ON ROBERT STREET EVERY DAY. AS LONG AS WE'RE TOGETHER, OUR MOTHERS SHOULD LET US GO OUT ON OUR OWN.

THAT WOULD BE...

A-HA!

WHA—

CERTAIN OLD LAMPS HAVE COPPER WIRE IN THEIR CORDS, WHICH IS EXACTLY WHAT I NEED...

SNIP

MY EXPERIMENT WAS AT A STANDSTILL...

MOTHER!!! I FOUND ONE!

DID YOU JUST CUT THE CORDS ON ALL OF THE LAMPS?

WHAT? OH, YES. THE WIRE IS HARD TO FIND.

THAT'S KINDA SHADY.

BUT TECHNICALLY, POSSESSION IS NINE-TENTHS OF THE LAW ... AND I HAVE DAMAGED PROPERTY.

WHAT ELSE, SHIRLEY?

THOSE THREE LAMPS AND THIS COAT.

WE'LL PAY FOR THOSE THREE LAMPS TOO, BUT WE WON'T BE TAKING THEM. THANK YOU.

DO YOU HAVE A PHONE?

YEAH. MY BROTHER SNUCK ME HIS OLD ONE.

WE'LL TRADE NUMBERS. I CAN SPEND TOMORROW AT THE COURTS IF THAT SUITS YOU.

ARE YOU AVAILABLE TOMORROW?

SORT OF ... I DON'T—

I'LL BE IN TOUCH.

Shirley Bones
+1-647-LHIQIY

SHIRLEY, LET'S GO!

WAIT! MY MOM'S NOT GOING TO LET—

JUST WAIT AND SEE.

JUST WAIT AND SEE ABOUT WHAT, JAMILA?

AMMI, I HONESTLY DON'T KNOW.

# Chapter 2

MOM!

"MOM"?! SINCE WHEN DO YOU CALL AMMI "MOM"?

FLASHBACK! TO THE MORNING BEFORE ...

I GUESS IT WAS FINALLY TIME FOR AMMI TO BRING UP THE TOPIC I'D BEEN AVOIDING: WHAT WAS GOING TO HAPPEN TO ME THIS SUMMER.

FAROOQ, YOU CALL ME AMMI. WE'RE NOT ON AN AMERICAN TELEVISION SHOW. AND YOU WILL NOT YELL IT, YOU WILL SPEAK RESPECTFULLY.

GROAAAN

MY BROTHER FAROOQ, AGE SIXTEEN.

BABY J! I DIDN'T EVEN SEE YOU THERE!

FAROOQ, DO YOU HAVE TIME FOR THIS?! YOU ARE WALKING!!

AMMI, FAROOQ GETS TO WALK. CAN'T I JUST—

AMMI, I AM SO FAST YOU DON'T EVEN KNOW. I CAN SPRINT THERE FASTER THAN CAPTAIN BRIEFCASE CAN DRIVE.

HEY!

THANKS FOR BREKKY, JJ! GOTTA JET!

AMMI!

HAVE A FRESH BOWL, JAMILA.

THANKS, AMMI.

YOU SEEM TO HAVE EVERYTHING UNDER CONTROL.

BARELY. YOU'RE WORKING LATE?

AND GOING IN EARLY FOR THE NEXT FEW WEEKS.

BUILDING SEASON.

KHUDA HAFIZ, JAMILA.

OBEY YOUR MOTHER. DON'T LISTEN TO FAROOQ.

I PROMISE I WON'T DO EITHER.

JAMILA. LISTEN TO YOUR MOTHER.

I KNOW! I WILL.

SLURRRP

AMMI, I PROMISE I WON'T **LOAF AROUND.** I WANT TO BE **OUTDOORS,** WHICH IS VERY HEALTHY, AND PHYSICALLY ACTIVE. LOTS OF **EXPERTS** THINK SPORTS ARE REALLY GOOD FOR BUILDING TEAM— UH, PLAYER-NESS AND—

JAMILA, IF YOU'RE AGAIN SUGGESTING THAT YOU PLAY BASKETBALL ALL SUMMER—

AMMI, WHY NOT?! FAROOQ GETS TO DO BASKETBALL CAMP AND I HAVE TO DO **SCIENCE**?! IT'S NOT FAIR!

YOUR BROTHERS WENT AT YOUR AGE, AND THEY **LOVED IT!**

YOU DO EXPERIMENTS! USE MICROSCOPES!

I JUST WANT TO PRACTICE ON A REAL COURT.

ABU PUT THE HOOP IN THE DRIVEWAY—

AND IT'S GREAT, BUT THERE'S A FULL-SIZED COURT ONLY FIVE BLOCKS AWAY!

FIVE LONG BLOCKS—

THEY AREN'T THAT LONG!

ACROSS A BUSY STREET—

THERE'S A CROSSWALK!

IN A NEW NEIGHBORHOOD—

IT WON'T BE NEW FOREVER!

BY YOURSELF?!

...

YOU DO WELL IN SCIENCE. I'D HAVE THOUGHT—

AMMI, I KNOW, I JUST DON'T WANT TO, OKAY?!

JAMILA WAHEED, THIS ATTITUDE! THERE IS A FUTURE IN SCIENCE, NOT BASKETBALL.

TAKE YOUR BOWL TO THE SINK AND GO TO YOUR ROOM.

I THOUGHT YOU DIDN'T WANT ME LOAFING AROUND THE HOUSE ALL DAY.

GO!

WE DIDN'T SPEAK AGAIN UNTIL THE NEXT DAY ... WHEN SHE TOLD ME WE WERE GOING TO A GARAGE SALE.

21

**Chapter 3**

FLASH FORWARD AGAIN.

RIIIING!

JAMILA, DO YOU HAVE MY PHONE?!

AFTER MEETING SHIRLEY, I DIDN'T REALLY THINK ANYTHING WOULD HAPPEN. SO WHEN THE PHONE RANG THE DAY AFTER WE MET, I HAD NO REASON TO SUSPECT THAT THINGS WERE ABOUT TO CHANGE.

NO! I'M OUTSIDE!

RIIIING!!!

DANG IT—AH! HERE IT IS— I FOUND IT!

DESPITE THE SCIENCE CAMP SHOW-DOWN, MY PARENTS ARE PRETTY GREAT. THE HOOP IS REALLY NICE OF THEM... BUT PLAYING ON A FULL-SIZED COURT IS THE DREAM.

AMMI! AMMI!

MY MOM DOESN'T GET IT.

THAT'S THE COURT I WANT TO PLAY ON! SEE! SEE HOW CLOSE IT IS?! SEE?!!

JAMILA, I'M DRIVING.

JAMILA! COME IN HERE PLEASE!

WHILE OUR MOTHERS DECIDED THE FATE OF OUR SUMMER, SHIRLEY AND I WAITED OUTSIDE AND WATCHED PEOPLE WALK BY.

THEY'RE COSPLAYERS.

AND **SHE** WORKS IN A CLOTHING STORE, BUT TODAY SHE GOT STUCK IN THE BACK ROOM. WHICH SHE HATES.

HUH?

YOU KNOW THEM, RIGHT?

I'VE NEVER SEEN ANY OF THESE PEOPLE BEFORE. BUT IT'S ALL TRUE.

PROVE IT!

OKAY.

25

THE SECOND CASE IS EVEN EASIER!

HER CLOTHES HAVE THE SAME BRAND TAG ON THEM. ODDS ARE THAT SHE WORKS THERE AND HAS TO WEAR THE CLOTHES SHE SELLS.

SHE HAS BLUE INK STAINS ON HER HANDS, LEG, AND SHIRT. THE TYPE OF INK THAT COMES FROM ANTI-THEFT TAGS THAT SOMETIMES BREAK WHEN YOU ARE STUCK IN THE BACK TAGGING CRATE AFTER CRATE OF CLOTHES.

OF COURSE SHE HATES IT. WHO WANTS TO SIT ALONE IN SOME ROOM GETTING COVERED IN INK?

EASY-PEASY.

PFFT. SUUUUUURE. WHATEVER.

29

THE GRAFFITI'S EASY: YOUR HANDS.

WHEN YOU WENT TO SHAKE HANDS I NOTICED SMUDGES ALONG THE SIDE OF YOUR HAND. SMUDGES JUST LIKE THE TYPE A PERMANENT MARKER MAKES ON A SLICK SURFACE...

LIKE A BATHROOM STALL.

DANG IT!

DANG IT AGAIN!

I GLANCED AT YOUR OTHER HAND: THAT CONFIRMED IT. THESE ARE THE SIGNATURE MARKS OF TRYING TO RECAP A MARKER IN HASTE. YOU MISS A FEW TIMES BEFORE YOU HIT THE CAP.

ALWAYS LOOK FOR THOSE MARKS ON THE NON-DOMINANT HAND: YOU'LL NEVER SEE A MARKER-USER WITHOUT THEM.

SO WHAT ARE YOU TROUBLEMAKERS DOING OUT HERE? LOITERING? TELLING FUTURES? SELLING KNIVES?

WELL...AMMI AND SHIRLEY'S MOM ARE INSIDE TALKING. ABOUT OUR SUMMER.

THERE'S NO WAY YOU'RE GETTING OUT OF SCIENCE CAMP, JJ.

I JUST CAN'T DO IT, FAROOQ. I CAN'T! I CAN'T! I ALREADY HAVE TO START AT A BRAND-NEW SCHOOL IN FALL...

WHOA! JJ!

AND SHE WANTS ME TO DO IT AGAIN NOW?!

SURELY THE KIDS AT SCIENCE CAMP WILL BE AT YOUR NEW SCHOOL ALSO?

ACTUALLY, NO. IT'S A FANCY CAMP THAT'S FULL OF PRIVATE SCHOOL KIDS.

YOU WENT?

YEAH. EVEN WHEN WE LIVED UPTOWN, OUR PARENTS SHELLED OUT MONEY WE DON'T HAVE & BUSED US OFF TO THIS "TOP RATED" CAMP.

SO OF COURSE I COULDN'T TELL THEM WHEN THE OTHER KIDS WERE...NOT GREAT.

WE HADN'T BEEN IN CANADA THAT LONG AND I STILL HAD AN ACCENT.

YES, FAROOQ?

UH...

PLUS AMMI AND ABU THOUGHT I SHOULD DRESS UP.

BUT HOW WAS THE CAMP? WHAT KINDS OF EXPERIMENTS DID YOU DO?

DON'T KNOW. ALL I REMEMBER IS TRYING TO GET THROUGH IT.

35

FINALLY...

SAHAR— IT'S BEEN A PLEASURE MEETING YOU. AND YOUR SON.

AND YOU, MATILDA. RAISING DAUGHTERS— ALWAYS AN ADVENTURE.

THE MOTHERS HAD SPOKEN.

ALL THAT WAS LEFT WAS THE VERDICT.

WHERE'S FAROOQ?

IN HIS ROOM.

JAMILA, SIT.

HERE WE GO AGAIN.

37

I'VE MADE A DECISION.

UH-OH.

I'VE DECIDED NOT TO ENROLL YOU IN SCIENCE CAMP—

ON THE CONDITION THAT YOU SPEND YOUR DAYS WITH SHIRLEY BONES AT THE BASKETBALL COURT FIVE BLOCKS AWAY.

WHAT?!

AMMI! DONE! YES! OF COURSE! YOU'RE THE BEST!

DON'T GET TOO EXCITED—THERE ARE RULES HERE.

YES OKAY SURE WHATEVER YOU SAY!

JAMILA, YOU ARE BOUNCING.

38

THE RULES WEREN'T BAD AT ALL.

1. JAMILA WILL SPEND HER SUMMER EITHER SUPERVISED BY A FAMILY MEMBER OR,
2. WITH SHIRLEY BONES IN THE FOLLOWING LOCATIONS ONLY:
   - AT THE BASKETBALL COURT ON ROBERT STREET
   - ON THE WAY TO OR FROM SAID COURT
   - EITHER GIRL'S BACKYARD (IN CASE OF RAIN, INDOORS ACCEPTABLE)
3. NO TV OR VIDEO GAMES.

DO WE HAVE AN AGREEMENT?

YES.

I WAS DYING TO KNOW WHAT CHANGED AMMI'S MIND, BUT DIDN'T WANT TO ASK IN CASE I BROKE THE SPELL.

WHEN DOES THIS AGREEMENT START?

MRS. BONES AND I AGREED ON TOMORROW.

TOMORROW!

TOMORROW

TOMORROW!

TOMORROW?

TOMORROW

TOMORROW

TOMO WORRA

TOMORROW

TOMORROW

TOMORROW

TOMORROW

ALWAYS USE THE CROSSWALKS — HIT THE BUTTON AND PUT YOUR ARM OUT TO LET DRIVERS KNOW YOU ARE CROSS-ING. CARS DON'T PAY ATTENTION! ESPECIALLY NOT TO CHILDREN. PROMISE ME YOU WILL NOT EVER JAYWALK. NEVER. ALWAYS WAIT FOR THE WALK LIGHT—EVEN IF THE LIGHT IS GREE... THERE COULD BE AN ARROW YOU CAN'T SEE, AND DRIVERS AREN'T LOOKING FOR—

41

YES...

"...THIS IS AN IMPROVEMENT."

IT WENT ON LIKE THIS FOR OVER A WEEK.

SHIRLEY WOULD PICK ME UP AT EIGHT AM.

SO PROMPT!

THANK YOU MRS. WAHEED.

WE'D WALK TO THE BASKETBALL COURTS.

I'D SHOOT HOOPS. SHE'D DO...WHATEVER.

MY THREE-POINTERS HAD NEVER BEEN BETTER.

WE DIDN'T TALK MUCH AT FIRST, BUT I COULD TELL SHIRLEY WAS JUST AS HAPPY AS I WAS WITH OUR ARRANGEMENT.

44

AT FIRST, I DIDN'T PAY MUCH ATTENTION...

BUT THEN I STARTED TO NOTICE THE KIDS.

A LOT OF KIDS SEEMED TO BE SHOWING UP AT THE COURT... TO MEET SHIRLEY.

SOMETIMES THEY'D BRING HER THINGS.

SOMETIMES SHE'D BRING THINGS FOR THEM.

45

AS THE DAYS WENT BY I GOT MORE AND MORE CURIOUS ABOUT MY NEW ... FRIEND? WE WEREN'T QUITE FRIENDS, BUT I DIDN'T KNOW A BETTER WORD.

IS THAT A CHEMISTRY BOOK?

OKAY, I CAN SEE THAT IT IS.

BUT HOW COME YOU'RE READING THAT?

IT LOOKS LIKE MY BROTHER'S FROM GRADE TEN.

IF GRADE FOUR SCIENCE BOOKS COVERED PH BALANCE, I'D READ **THEM**.

...

SHE DIDN'T GIVE UP MUCH INFORMATION.

47

48

I COULDN'T MAKE SENSE OF MY NEW COMPANION.

SOMETIMES SHE WAS CHATTY ENOUGH AND WOULD TELL ME ALL KINDS OF THINGS.

AND SOMETIMES IT WAS OBVIOUS SHE DIDN'T WALK TO TALK.

SHE SEEMED TO BE THINKING REALLY HARD.

OR NOT AT ALL.

BUT I WAS THERE TO PLAY BALL. SO I TRIED TO ACCEPT I MIGHT NEVER KNOW MORE ABOUT HER.

THEN, THIS ONE DAY,
THINGS CHANGED.

AH HOO-HOO-HOO

SNIFF
SNIFF

51

HEY. WHAT'S GOING ON?

SHE WON'T HELP ME.

NOT WON'T—CAN'T.

JAMILA, THIS IS OLIVER.

BUT YOU WON'T—

CAN'T HELP— IT WOULD REQUIRE LEAVING THE COURTS AND BREAKING OUR MOTHERS' RULES.

OH.

ENOCH IS MISSING!

WHO'S ENOCH?

HIS LIZARD.

GECKO. WE HAVE TO GO NOW.

IT'S NOT THAT FAR, I SWEAR.

HE'S ALONE AND MISSING.

HE COULD BE DEAD.

PLEASE HELP ME! IF HE'S HURT...

# Chapter 5

SO, WHERE ARE WE GOING?

TO CHRISTIE PITS.

COME ON!

THE PARK?

THE POOL AT THE PARK.

WE WON'T HAVE TO SWIM, WILL WE? BECAUSE I DON'T HAVE MY—

WE WON'T BE SWIMMING.

INHALE

EXHALE

WHY DON'T YOU JUST TELL ME WHAT THIS IS ALL ABOUT.

55

SO, WHY NOT BE MORE CAREFUL WITH YOUR STUFF, THEN?

ARE YOU SERIOUS?

THAT'S THE THING I'M TRYING TO TELL YOU.

SURE, WE PROB'LY LOST SOME JUNK, BUT THIS ISN'T THAT.

OUR STUFF IS BEING STOLEN.

57

60

SO, HOW DID HE—

HE KNEW TO COME TO ME BECAUSE THIS IS THE TYPE OF THING I DO.

ANIMAL WRANGLING?!

*SNT*
HA-HA NO—

HA HA HA HA HA HA HA HA

YOU DONE?

62

IT WASN'T A FAVOR. IT WASN'T CHARITY OR FOR MORAL OR ETHICAL REASONS. IT WAS LOGICAL FOR HER TO HELP ME.

THE THING THAT'S UNIQUE ABOUT HER IS SHE COULD SEE I NEEDED HELP ... AND SHE SAW NOT ONLY HOW TO GET IT BUT HOW IT COULD HELP HER TOO.

SHIRLEY DIDN'T CARE THAT SHE DIDN'T KNOW ME OR THAT MY PARENTS ARE STRICT.

IN FACT, SHE USED ALL OF THAT INFORMATION TO MAKE A BETTER SOLUTION.

I DON'T KNOW WHAT THAT MAKES HER BUT SINCE HUMANS ARE ANIMALS, MAYBE "ANIMAL WRANGLER" IS ACTUALLY PRETTY CLOSE.

I'M A DETECTIVE.

SERIOUSLY?

UH-HUH.

COOL!

IT'S FAIRLY ORDINARY.

NO, IT'S NOT.

SO YOU SOLVE CRIMES?!

I'M TEN. THE POLICE ARE NOT CALLING ME UP TO DEAL WITH A BANK ROBBERY.

BUT YOU'VE SEEN FOR YOURSELF: KIDS OFTEN HAVE PROBLEMS THAT ADULTS CAN'T OR WON'T SOLVE.

HURRY!

BUT HOW DID OLIVER **KNOW** ABOUT YOU?

THE WORD GETS AROUND.

ELABORATE, PLEASE.

IT STARTED AT SCHOOL...

WHAT ARE YOU DOING TONIGHT?!

I'M PLAYING MY NEW GAME AND—

I'LL BE STUDYING FOR THE SCIENCE QUIZ TOMORROW.

WHAT? THERE'S NO QUIZ.

DON'T LISTEN TO WEIRDO.

YOU DON'T HAVE TO BELIEVE ME.

GIGGLE!

GIGGLE!

SNORT!

IT'S TRUE REGARDLESS. BUT BY ALL MEANS, FILL YOUR EVENING WITH DRECK.

WHATEVER, WEIRDO.

NO, WAIT.

WHAT'S DRECK?

WHO CARES?!

SHIRLEY, WHY DO YOU THINK THERE'S A QUIZ?

THERE **WILL** BE A QUIZ.

I LEARNED IT FROM WATCHING MS. DUGGS.

TODAY, SHE PULLED SOMETHING OUT OF THE RED FILE—

WHAT RED FILE?

WHAT ARE YOU EVEN DOING IN CLASS?

MS. D HAS FILED TESTS IN THE SAME RED FILE SEVEN TIMES THIS YEAR.

SO? MAYBE SHE'S JUST FILING.

AND I SUPPOSE THAT'S WHY SHE HANDED ONE SHEET TO THE SECRETARY TO MAKE TWENTY-NINE COPIES— ONE FOR EVERY KID IN THE CLASS . . .

BY TOMORROW BEFORE TEN AM PLEASE.

MS. DUGGS NEEDS HER COPIES BY TEN AM.

BETWEEN TEN AND LUNCH WE HAVE TWO SUBJECTS:

SCIENCE AND LANGUAGE ARTS. WE JUST HAD A TEST IN LANGUAGE ARTS EIGHT DAYS AGO.

TOMORROW WE'RE HAVING A POP QUIZ. IN SCIENCE.

SINCE MICHAYLA WAS SICK FOR TWO DAYS...

AND GABRIELLA, YOU AND SHAY PASSED NOTES FOR THE LAST THREE SCIENCE LESSONS...

(AND YOU BOTH GET C'S IN SCIENCE)...

YOU MAY WANT TO STUDY.

THE NEXT DAY

OKAY CLASS. HOLD ON TO YOUR BUTTS: IT'S A POP QUIZ!

Chapter 6

WE'RE ALMOST THERE!

NO RUNNING.

FINALLY!

OLIVER! I'VE BEEN WAITING 'N' WATCHING EVERYONE HERE FOR AGES!!

AND THAT'S MY SISTER.

75

OKAY, THE MISSING ITEM IS A BACKPACK: DESCRIBE IT TO ME.

IT'S NAVY BLUE,

WITH A MESH COMPARTMENT.

WOULDN'T ENOCH GET SQUISHED IN THERE?

NO, IT'S FOAM THAT HOLDS ITS SHAPE. THE MESH PART IS LIKE A LITTLE GECKO APARTMENT!

THOSE ARE OUR TOWELS.

SO, WHAT ARE YOU GOING TO **DO**?

FIRST, FIND OUT WHAT "THE PROFESSIONALS" KNOW.

TOBY'S OKAY, BUT LESTRAD'S A REAL JERK.

79

BUT VEE SAID SHE'S BEEN HERE THIS WHOLE DAY. DIDN'T YOU SEND PEOPLE HOME TODAY?

LOOK, PEOPLE GET REAL MAD WHEN YOU SEND 'EM HOME.

AFTER KUMI SHOUTED, I CLEARED THE POOLS, AND WENT TO GET A CLOSER LOOK BEFORE EVACUATING THE WHOLE PLACE AND GETTING GRIPED AT BY EVERYBODY.

KIDS ARE ALWAYS THROWIN' STUFF IN THERE, PULLING DUMB PRANKS, WASTING OUR TIME. IT LOOKED MORE LIKE CANDY THAN **YOU KNOW WHAT**.

SO I LET EVERYONE STAY WHILE I SKIMMED IT.

I WAS RIGHT, IT WAS A CHOCOLATE, SO EVERYONE GOT BACK IN. DONEZO.

DONEZO INDEED.

VEE AND OLIVER COME HERE EVERY DAY—I BET YOU KNOW THEM PRETTY WELL.

SURE. I MEAN—I'M NOT A BABYSITTER. I'M HERE TO **SAVE LIVES**.

BUT YEAH, I SEE THEM EVERY DAY.

SO YOU KNOW THEY'VE BEEN GETTING THEIR THINGS STOLEN?

HEY. DON'T DISTRACT THE LIFEGUARDS, KID.

TAP TAP TAP

WE'RE NOT HERE TO BABYSIT, WE'RE HERE TO **SAVE LIVES**.

SO I HEAR. SINCE YOU'RE SO VIGILANT, I BET YOU'VE SEEN VEE AND OLIVER'S STUFF GETTING STOLEN ALL SUMMER.

GETTING **LOST** YOU MEAN. I'VE SEEN THOSE KIDS DRAGGING THEIR WHOLE TOY BOX TO THE POOL. KIDS LOSE THINGS. WHEN YOU'RE MY AGE, YOU'LL SEE.

I'M SURE I WILL.

SOUNDS LIKE YOU SEE A LOT: DID YOU SEE THE NEAR-"FOUL POOL" TODAY?

TAP TAP TAP

85

KUMI OKADA IS TWELVE. SHE'S THE TALLEST KID IN HER CLASS AND THE MEANEST. GOOD GRADES, BUT BAD ATTITUDE. "DOES NOT MEET EXPECTATIONS" FOR STUFF LIKE CLASS PARTICIPATION, SMILING, AND NOT BEING A GRUMPY JERK.

SHOVE!!

KUMI?

KUMI?

AND SHE WAS HERE THIS MORNING, CALLED FOUL POOL AND WAS GONE BEFORE YOU NOTICED YOUR BACKPACK WAS MISSING.

WHAT ARE YOU SMILING ABOUT?

THE CHASE IS ON!

AND THEN WE WAITED, WHILE SHIRLEY "EXAMINED THE SCENE."

I WAS BEGINNING TO REALIZE THAT EVERYTHING SHIRLEY DID HAD SOME BIGGER POINT ... BUT NOT EVERYONE WAS GETTING IT ...

SHIRLEY'S SO WEIRD. THIS IS NOT GONNA GET ENOCH BACK!

IT WILL! SHIRLEY HELPED MY FRIEND KAI'S OLDER SISTER'S FRIEND AND SHE TOLD HER, WHO TOLD KAI, WHO TOLD ME THAT SHIRLEY BONES CAN DO **ANYTHING!**

SHE'S CRAWLING AROUND SOME TOWELS LIKE A WORM.

A **GENIUS WORM.** YOU WAIT AND SEE, VEE.

PBBTTT!

PBBBTT

SPLASH

OH YEAH?!

SPLASH!

I'LL DESTROY YOU!

NO!

SHUT YOUR FACE!

YOU!

YOU!

89

SHH!

TWEEEEEEEEEEEEEEEEEEEEEEEET!

KEEP IT DOWN!

COOL IT WITH THAT WHISTLE!

YOU KIDS GET OUT OF HERE! YOU'RE DONE!!

BUT NO BUT—YOU—NO! BUT—NO, BUT! YOU CAN'T! WAIT, THOUGH!

I CAN AND I HAVE. YOU ARE BANNED.

...HE HAD NOT FORGOTTEN.

I'M ALL THROUGH, LET'S GO.

BUT SHIRLEY DIDN'T SEEM THAT BOTHERED AT ALL.

FINE. THREE DAYS. THAT'S IT, THOUGH.

OR WHAT?! SHE'S **HELPING** YOU! IF SHE DOESN'T, YOU'LL STILL BE BANNED AND IT WILL HAVE BEEN YOUR OWN FAULT!

YOU STAY OUT OF IT, JAYLA!

IT'S **JAMILA**. AND I'M IN IT WHETHER YOU LIKE IT OR NOT.

I HAVE TO BE HOME FOR TEA SOON. I'LL BE IN TOUCH.

YOU BETTER.

SH!

OF ALL THE UNGRATEFUL...

WOW, THAT WAS SOMETHING!

ENOCH BACK IN THREE DAYS?

YOU'RE NOT REALLY AS SURE AS YOU'RE PRETENDING, RIGHT?

THREE DAYS SHOULD BE MORE THAN SUFFICIENT ... TO GET ENOCH BACK ANYWAY.

HOW DO WE CATCH KUMI?

I HAVE A FEW RESOURCES ...

HEY! WHERE ARE YOU GOING? I THOUGHT WE WERE GOING HOME.

WE ARE.

WE'RE JUST TAKING THE LONG WAY.

YOU COMING?

WHAT TIME IS IT, MR. WOLF?!

THREE O'CLOCK!

**Chapter 7**

A QUICK BLOCK LATER...

A DAYCARE?

YOU WANT TO TALK TO SOME KIDS?

THE DAYCARE IS CRUCIAL.

SARA TARIN IS SORT OF IN CHARGE— HER FAMILY RUNS THE DAYCARE AND SHE KNOWS ALL THE REGULARS.

HOW WOULD DAYCARE KIDS HELP?

IT'S WHAT THE GROWN-UPS SAY WHEN THEY DON'T THINK THE KIDS ARE LISTENING.

KIDS ARE THE BEST SPIES, BECAUSE EVERYONE UNDERESTIMATES WHAT THEY UNDERSTAND... AND REMEMBER.

THIS KID STILL NEEDED A STOOL TO BRUSH HER TEETH. HOW COULD SHE HELP?

HER BABY BROTHERS GET BRUNG HERE SOMETIMES.

WHAT DID YOU HEAR?

SOUNDS LIKE THE SCHOOL CALLS A LOT.

HOW'S IT GOING WITH KUMI?

YOU KNOW. IT'S HARD.

KUMI'S A BULLY?

KUMI GETS BULLIED. OR SHE DID.

KIDS CAN BE SO CRUEL.

ISN'T THAT THE TRUTH?

OUR KUMI DOESN'T LIKE MANY PEOPLE. UNLESS THEY'RE CHARACTERS IN SOME DRAGON BOOK.

AT LEAST SHE'S READING.

OH, HER GRADES AREN'T A PROBLEM...

SHE JUST WANTED TO KEEP TO HERSELF!

WOOOOW.

I THINK SHE SOUNDS PRETTY AWESOME.

ABSOLUTELY.

OLIVER AND VEE WERE GETTING IN HER WAY! D'YOU THINK TAKING THE BACKPACK WAS HER "SHOVE"?

WE DON'T KNOW KUMI TOOK THE BACKPACK.

BUT VEE AND OLIVER—

IT'S FATAL TO DRAW CONCLUSIONS BEFORE COLLECTING ALL OF THE EVIDENCE.

YEAH, YOU SAID THA—

KNOW WHERE KUMI LIVES?

YEAH. YELLOW HOUSE ON THE CORNER. TWO BLOCKS OVER.

ANY WORD ON A GECKO?

OH RIGHT!

HMM. PETS... PETS...

HUDA'S SISTER'S GOT A TROPICAL FISH TANK...

PRIYA GUPTA'S PARENTS ARE GETTING HER A PUPPY. I HEARD A RUMOR ABOUT A COUPLA TURTLES AT THE BOMBERRYS'.

BUT NO GECKOS. YET.

KEEP ME POSTED, OKAY? I'VE GOT MORE IF YOU HEAR ANYTHING. I'LL COME BY WHEN I CAN.

I'M HERE FROM NINE TO FIVE THIRTY.

WHAT ABOUT A CHOMPO BAR?

NO, I'M A FIVE-CENT CANDY KID MYSELF.

ANY KIDS YOU KNOW GO FOR CHOMPOS?

HA! LIKE THE ONE IN THE POOL TODAY?

YEAH! HOW DID YOU KNOW?

HALF THE POOL WALKS PAST HERE. EVERYONE WAS TALKING.

ANYONE LOVE CHOMPOS AS MUCH AS YOU LOVE FIVE-CENT CANDIES?

HUH. LEMME THINK—

AC'SHULLY YEAH!

HEY RIZAL!

COME 'ERE!

NADEEM C. EATS CHOMPOS BUT SHE'S AWAY AT CAMP.

RIZ, WHO EATS CHOMPOS ALL THE TIME?

THERE WAS THAT ONE KID, BUT SHE GOT SICK AND I THINK MOVED OR SUMPTHIN'.

WHAT ABOUT FELIX?

SNACK TIME!

YEAH! FELIX GARNEAU EATS CHOMPOS! RAISINETTES TOO, BUT CHOMPOS MOSTLY! I THINK THEY'RE AT THEIR DAD'S THIS WEEK.

SMACK!

I'LL KEEP MY EARS OP—

SARA! SNACK!

I GOTTA GO! SOMETIMES IT'S HALF AN APPLE, BUT I HEAR TODAY IT'S ICE CREAM!

TELL THE OTHERS: THERE'S CANDY FOR ANYONE WITH INFO ON KUMI, GECKOS, AND CHOMPO BARS!

DAYCARE KIDS, HUH?

TAR IN DAYCARE

I HAD TO ADMIT I WAS IMPRESSED. SARA AND THE DAYCARE KIDS WERE EVERYTHING SHIRLEY PROMISED.

109

YOU KNOW WHOSE THIS IS?! GREAT! **YOU TAKE IT!**

HEY!

I WAS JUST ON MY WAY BACK TO THE POOL TO DROP IT IN THE LOST-AND-FOUND.

BUT I THOUGHT—

TELL ME EVERYTHING!

I HAVE TWIN BABY BROTHERS, SO MY HOUSE IS FULL OF SCREAMS. MY PARENTS LET ME GO TO THE POOL TO GET AWAY SO I'LL BE "SUPERVISED."

AS IF THOSE TEENAGED BROKEN PENCILS ARE EVEN PAYING ATTENTION.

THEY DIDN'T EVEN SEE THE TURD IN THE POOL!

HELLO?!!

YES, **YOU** FIRST SPOTTED THE "FOUL POOL."

SOME DISGUSTING BABY PROBABLY DROPPED THEIR DRAWERS—I GET ENOUGH OF THAT AT HOME.

WAAAAH. WAHHHHHH! WAAAAH WAHH! WAHHHH! WAHH AAH! WAHHH!

SO YOU LEFT?

I WASN'T STICKING AROUND TO WATCH THEM POKE POOP WITH A SKIMMER.

I GRABBED MY STUFF AND WENT TO THE LIBRARY.

SHE LEFT BEFORE THEY KNEW THE DOODY WAS FAKE.

SO YOU GRABBED THE WRONG BACKPACK BY MISTAKE?

GROSS!

OOH!

CLEAR THE POOLS!

EVERYONE STAND BACK!

CLEAR ALL POOLS!

I HAD **MY** BACKPACK.

UNTIL ...

OOF!

I HAD IT ALL WRONG.

WHAT? OH, YES. YOU DID.

SO, MY QUESTION:

THE GIRL: IN WHICH DIRECTION DID SHE RUN?

ALONG BARTON STREET, TOWARD THE CONVENIENCE STORE.

EAST.

IT REALLY IS GETTING LATE—WE BOTH SHOULD GET HOME.

YOU'RE TAKING ENOCH?

YES. I'LL LET OLIVER AND VEE KNOW HE'S SAFE.

WHAT ABOUT **MY** BAG?

I DON'T KNOW. YET.

SHIRLEY GOT KUMI'S CONTACT INFORMATION AND WE HEADED HOME.

I CAN'T BELIEVE IT WASN'T KUMI AFTER ALL!

THE MATCHING BACKPACK WAS A TRICKY COINCIDENCE.

WHAT AN EXCEPTIONAL CASE!

THE MORE I THINK ABOUT IT, THE MORE QUESTIONS I HAVE!

YOU SUM UP THE IMPORTANT QUESTIONS VERY WELL.

WHO IS THIS MYSTERY KID?

HOW DID SHE GET OLIVER'S BACKPACK?

DID SHE TAKE IT ON PURPOSE?

IF SHE DID, WHY?

WHY DID SHE RUN FROM KUMI?

WHERE DID SHE GO?

AND HOW DO WE FIND HER?

Chapter 8

JAMILA, IS THAT YOU?

YES, AMMI!

GIVE ME A HAND WITH THESE PICTURES.

OOOOO, FANCY HOUSE.

YOU THINK EVERYTHING NICE IS "FANCY."

WELL, IT IS.

WHAT'S THIS?

A LIE DETECTOR.

WHAT?

118

I BET IT DOESN'T WORK ON HUMANS, BUT THE DAY I BROKE THE RULES WAS NOT A GOOD DAY TO TEST IT.

IT'S REALLY CALLED A LIE DETECTOR?

HA-HA NO, I WAS TEASING. IT'S CALLED A LEVEL.

WHEW.

WEIRD NAME.

BECAUSE IT TELLS IF THINGS ARE LEVEL TO THE GROUND.

UNLIKE NOW.

121

BACK IN MY ROOM, I WAS PROBABLY SUPPOSED TO BE THINKING ABOUT WHAT I'D DONE WRONG...

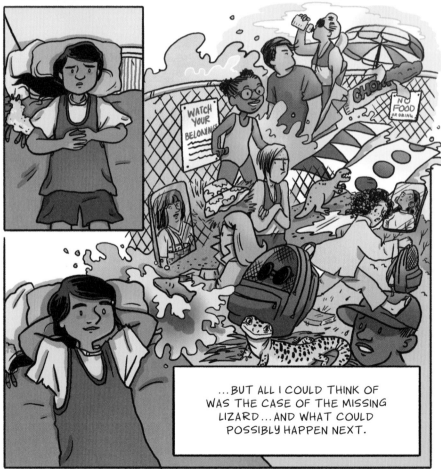

...BUT ALL I COULD THINK OF WAS THE CASE OF THE MISSING LIZARD...AND WHAT COULD POSSIBLY HAPPEN NEXT.

# Chapter 9

TENSE DINNER. TENSE SLEEP. TENSE BREAKFAST.

FAROOQ! SIT AND EAT!

AMMI, I'M GOING TO BE LATE!

YOU ALWAYS HAVE TIME FOR YOUR FRIENDS! MAKE TIME FOR YOUR FAMILY!

THIS IS YOUR FAULT.

I KNOW.

NAVEED!

HE'S ALREADY GONE.

ABU TOO.

IS THAT SO.

YUP. THANKS FOR BREAKFAST, AMMI! BYE!

NOOOOOOOOO.

SOOOOOOORRY.

I...

JAMILA!

AH!

BRING ME A BANANA!

GET IT YOURSELF!

I JUST LACED UP MY SHOES!

DON'T YOU COME IN THE HOUSE WITH YOUR SHOES ON!

JAMILA, BRING YOUR BROTHER A BANANA.

I KNOW, BUT SHE LISTENED THIS ONE TIME. SO MAYBE SHE WILL AGAIN...?

WHY'D YOU SNEAK OFF ANYWAY? YOU KNOW AMMI'S THE WORLD'S BEST DETECTIVE.

HA! NOT ANYMORE.

THERE WAS THIS KID WHO NEEDED SHIRLEY'S HELP... AND MINE, I GUESS.

SEE! IT'S NOT LIKE YOU TO SNEAK OFF FOR PRANKS

(LIKE I WOULD HAVE).

TELL HER THAT!

I TRIED YESTERDAY!

I KNOW, BUT SHE'S COOLED OFF BY NOW.

I GOTTA GO. I REALLY AM LATE.

SMACK

TRY HER AGAIN!

HEY!

129

SO I WENT IN TO TRY AGAIN...

AMMI?

...AND TO THROW OUT A BANANA PEEL.

I TOLD HER WHAT HAPPENED...

OLIVER WAS SO SCARED!

AND SHE REALLY LISTENED.

SHE TOLD ME WHY SHE GOT SO MAD—MOSTLY BECAUSE SHE WAS SCARED, BOTH THAT I MIGHT NOT BE SAFE BUT ALSO THAT I WAS TURNING INTO A KID WHO LIES.

YEAH!

I DIDN'T WANT TO LIE!

—BUT YOU HAD TO CHOOSE BETWEEN RULES AND HELPING.

AMMI LOOKS TIRED SOMETIMES.

THESE ARE THE KIND OF CHOICES YOU MAKE AS YOU GROW UP. I—

DING-DONG ♪

I'LL GET IT.

DING-DONG! ♪

I FORGOT TO TELL SHIRLEY BONES ABOUT ...

HELLO, MRS. WAHEED. I'M HERE TO...

= CLICK

JAMILA—

YES AMMI?

THAT WAS FAST!

SHIRLEY BONES IS OUTSIDE WAITING FOR YOU.

I KNOW. I'M SORRY. I FORGOT TO TELL HER WE COULDN'T SPEND TIME TOGETHER ANYMORE.

NO. I MEAN GET YOUR BALL AND GO ON—YOU CAN JOIN HER.

WHAT? ARE YOU SURE?! HOW ... WHAT—

JAMILA, DO YOU WANT TO GO OR NOT?

...

YES, OF COURSE! THANK YOU, AMMI!

BEFORE YOU LEAVE ...

I WANT TO AMEND OUR AGREEMENT.

SCREECH

AMMI CALLED MRS. BONES AND THEY AGREED ON A PERIMETER THAT SHIRLEY AND I HAD TO STAY WITHIN.

YOU CAN USE FAROOQ'S OLD PHONE TO STAY IN TOUCH ONLY. HE'LL FIND IT FOR YOU TONIGHT. YOU CAN USE SHIRLEY'S PHONE TODAY.

FAROOQ'S PHONE, ALREADY IN MY POCKET.

YES, AMMI.

133

# Chapter 10

NOW GO. AND HAVE FUN.

THANK YOU, AMMI.

WHEW.

I TOLD HER WHAT HAPPENED AND SHE REALLY LISTENED!

SHE SAID I CAN HAVE A PHONE! IT'S FAROOQ'S THAT I ALREADY HAVE, BUT STILL!

NOW I WON'T HAVE TO HIDE IT! AND WE CAN GO FARTHER FROM THE COURTS, WE JUST HAVE TO TELL OUR MOMS ...

HEY, WHERE ARE WE GOING?

I'M INVESTIGATING.

YOU ARE? DON'T YOU MEAN WE?

OKAY, FINE.

WHAT ARE YOU INVESTIGATING TODAY.

THE SAME CASE.

I'VE BEEN DYING TO KNOW:

WHERE'S ENOCH? AND OLIVER'S BACKPACK?!

THEY PICKED IT UP.

WHO?

VEE AND OLIVER

WHEN?

LAST NIGHT.

AND?

AND WHAT?

AND WHAT'S THE NEXT MOVE? DO YOU HAVE NEW LEADS ON FINDING KUMI'S BACKPACK?

AND WHAT ABOUT THE HAT?!

DID YOU **DEDUCE** ANYTHING FROM THAT?

SHIRLEY.

MM?

SHIRLEY, WHAT ARE WE DOING?

I **TOLD YOU.** INVESTIGATING.

YES, **WHAT**, THOUGH?

137

I'M GOING.

IF YOU CAN JUST WAIT FOR—

FOR WHAT?! FOR THE REST OF THE DAY WHILE YOU GRUNT TWO WORDS AT ME AND WON'T TELL ME ANYTHING?!

NO, I CAN'T.

YOU KNOW WHAT?

YOU ONLY CARE ABOUT ANYONE IF THEY CAN HELP YOU.

IF I GO HOME YOU HAVE TO GO TOO. THAT'S THE ONLY REASON YOU WANT ME TO STAY. TO GET YOUR CASE. YOUR WAY.

145

ALL RIGHT.

WHEW!

FWUMP

THUMP THUMP THUMP THUMP

SWISH

SWISH

SHRUG

JAMILA, WHERE IS SHIRLEY?

I DON'T KNOW. AT HER HOUSE, PROBABLY.

WHY ISN'T SHE WITH YOU?

WE HAD A FIGHT.

WELL, GO MAKE UP, THEN. I'M WORKING FROM HOME—YOU CAN'T BE BANGING IN THE DRIVEWAY ALL DAY.

I COULDN'T PLAY WITH SHIRLEY. NOW I COULDN'T EVEN PLAY IN MY OWN DRIVEWAY.

I WAS ACTUALLY WORSE OFF THAN I STARTED.

AT LEAST I WASN'T AT SCIENCE CAMP.

BUT HOW LONG BEFORE AMMI BROUGHT THAT UP AGAIN?

I NEEDED TO FIX THIS NOW.

BUT HOW?

149

I WONDERED WHAT SHIRLEY WOULD DO.

...FIVE SECONDS BEFORE I REMEMBERED I WAS MAD AT HER.

BESIDES, THE THING I ~~LIKE~~ **USED** TO LIKE ABOUT HER IS HOW I COULDN'T GUESS HER NEXT MOVE.

SHE SURPRISED ME.

I COULDN'T GET INTO HER HEAD IF I WANTED TO.

WHICH I DIDN'T WANT TO BECAUSE SHE WAS MEAN AND A JERK AND BOSSY AND KEPT SECRETS AND—

RRRR!

UH...

OH.

SORRY.

IS IT WORTH IT FOR SHIRLEY?

I NEEDED TO KNOW MORE.

I NEEDED...

EVIDENCE.

155

COUGH

CAN I HELP YOU WITH SOMETHING, JAMILA?

OKAY. I CAN TELL YOU A LITTLE BIT.

PLEASE FORGIVE THE MESS. WE'RE STILL SETTLING IN.

I APOLOGIZE FOR THE SHORT NOTICE.

SHIRLEY WAS QUITE INSISTENT THAT I CALL AS SOON AS POSSIBLE.

...I TOO WAS EAGER TO SPEAK WITH YOU ABOUT THE GIRLS' SUMMER.

JAMILA IS GOING TO SCIENCE CAMP.

YES, I HAVE SHIRLEY REGISTERED FOR A DANCE CAMP...

BUT IT SEEMS NEITHER GIRL IS DELIGHTED WITH THEIR PROSPECTS.

MRS. WAHEED, I DON'T WISH TO INTERFERE...

EXCEPT...

HM.

MAY I TELL YOU A BIT ABOUT OUR SHIRLEY?

YES, PLEASE GO ON.

SHE'S VERY BRIGHT...
BUT SOCIALLY...SCHOOL
YARDS ARE RATHER
UNKIND PLACES.

WEIRDO!
WEIRDO!
WEIRDO!
WEIRDO!
WEIRDO!
WEIRDO!
WEIRDO!
WEIRDO!

AND PLAY DATES HAVE BEEN...
FRANKLY, DISASTROUS.

WHAT'S
THAT FOR?

WHY ARE
YOU LOOKING
AT THAT?

WHAT ARE
YOU DOING?

AAAAAAAAA!

I'M GOING
HOME!

MY DEAR, WHAT
HAPPENED?!

SHIRLEY
TURNED MY
DRESS BLUE!

IT'S INVISIBLE
INK...ONCE IT
DRIES, ANYWAY.

THANK YOU FOR
COMING BY.

160

SLAM!

WHAT'S WRONG DEAR?

A-HUR HUR HURRR

SHIRLEY... IS MEAN! I'M GOING HOME!

WHAT? SHE PICKED "ACCOUNTANT" AND CAN'T EVEN ADD!

...YES, I MENTIONED IT, BUT I THOUGHT SHE'D **KNOW** THE DIVORCE RATE CONSIDERING HER PARENTS...

THAT GIRL IS **WEIRD**.

A REAL KNOW-IT-ALL...AND A **JERK**.

WOULDN'T PLAY DREAM PHONE, WOULDN'T WATCH TV, WOULDN'T LOOK AT MAGAZINES...

SHE **CHEATS**. CHESS, CHECKERS, CLUE, STRATEGO... SHE **CHEATS**.

I'M GOING HOME!

I'M GOING HOME!

I'M GOING HOME!

I'M GOING HOME!

THE JUMBLE SALE WAS THE FIRST TIME I'VE SEEN SHIRLEY MAKE A FRIEND.

SHIRLEY CAN BE ... DIFFICULT. HER PERCEPTIVENESS IMPEDES HER ABILITY TO SOCIALIZE. BUT IT IS ALSO A GIFT.

SHE SEES SOMETHING IN JAMILA.

AND JAMILA SEEMS TO SEE SOMETHING IN HER. SO I WONDERED IF THEY COULD SPEND SOME TIME TOGETHER.

IT'S A RISK—AN EXPERIMENT: GIVE THEM SOME FREEDOM—

AND SEE IF THEY CAN LEARN SOMETHING FROM EACH OTHER THAT NEITHER COULD FROM DAY CAMP.

YES!

# Chapter 12

♪ DING-DONG

THE NEXT MORNING, AFTER THE BOYS HAD ALL LEFT:

WELL, GO GET IT!

RIGHT.

I'M SO SORRY!

HOW COULD YOU?!

YOU'RE GOING DOWN.

LET'S TALK.

COME TO THE BACKYARD.

SHIRLEY, I'M SORRY I CALLED YOU A WE—

HERE'S WHAT I CAN DO:

I WILL AGREE TO A SCHEDULE OF HALF BASKETBALL, HALF CASE WORK.

ON THE CONDITION THAT YOU CAN BE FLEXIBLE, SINCE CRIME KNOWS NO SCHEDULE.

IF A PARTICULARLY FASCINATING CASE COMES UP THAT TAKES SEVERAL DAYS, I WILL MAKE UP THE TIME ON THE COURT. DEAL?

ACTUALLY ... I— I DON'T MIND ...

I LIKE THE CASE WORK.

BUT YOU GOTTA TELL ME WHAT'S GOING ON. I WON'T BE SOME SILENT SIDEKICK ...

I WANT IN AND I WANT TO HELP ... IF I CAN.

I ... THINK I CAN DO THAT.

HEY. UM. I'M GLAD YOU CAME OVER. I WAS SCARED TO CALL—

THERE'S ALWAYS READING I CAN DO WHEN WE'RE AT THE COURTS. I'M RESEARCHING DIFFERENT TYPES OF SOIL...

UH...

I...SEEM TO THINK BETTER WHEN YOU ARE AROUND.

IT'S A NEW EXPERIENCE I HAVE NOT STUDIED EXTENSIVELY BEFORE.

WHAT IS?

168

I WAS DYING TO ASK SHIRLEY MORE QUESTIONS,

BUT I KEPT MY PROMISE TO WAIT FOR HER BIG REVEAL.

Chapter 13

WE TOOK THE SAME ROUTE WE TOOK TO THE POOL THE FIRST DAY WE MET OLIVER.

172

175

GULP

THAT EXPLAINS IT! MY NEIGHBOR'S DOG GOT LOOSE AND THE HAT TURNED UP IN MY YARD.

SO KIND OF YOU KIDS TO BRING IT BACK! HOW DID YOU FIND US?

ME! UM. I... RECOGNIZED THE HAT. I GO TO THE POOL MOST DAYS AND WALK PAST YOUR HOUSE. I... UH... SEE YOU IN THE SPRINKLER SOMETIMES.

INVITE US IN BEFORE SHE ASKS MORE QUESTIONS.

WELL, ISN'T THAT—

WOULD YOU LIKE TO COME IN? MOM, IMA— CAN THEY COME IN AND PLAY?

OH! UH ... OF COURSE. ALL OF YOU ... ARE WEL—

COME TO THE BACKYARD.

SUNSCREEN!

I KNOW!

OKAY. WHO ARE YOU AND WHAT IS GOING ON?

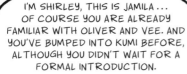

I'M SHIRLEY, THIS IS JAMILA ... OF COURSE YOU ARE ALREADY FAMILIAR WITH OLIVER AND VEE. AND YOU'VE BUMPED INTO KUMI BEFORE, ALTHOUGH YOU DIDN'T WAIT FOR A FORMAL INTRODUCTION.

AND **YOU** ARE ANGIE MALINOWSKI.

PEOPLE MAKE THIS FACE A LOT AFTER TALKING TO SHIRLEY.

YOU'VE BEEN SICK, CANCER OF SOME KIND, AND YOU'RE FINALLY GETTING BETTER.

YOU'VE BEEN SNEAKING OUT WHEN YOUR PARENTS ARE AT WORK.

YOU WEAR LONG SLEEVES AND A HAT SO THEY WON'T NOTICE A TAN.

YOU'VE BEEN HANGING AROUND OUTSIDE THE POOL, STEALING FROM OLIVER AND VEE, UNDETECTED...

...UNTIL YOU GOT A BIG PRIZE: THE BACKPACK WITH THE LIZARD INSIDE!

GECKO!

YOU ALMOST ESCAPED... EXCEPT YOU RAN INTO KUMI AND ACCIDENTALLY SWITCHED BAGS.

WHAT? HOW DO YOU KNOW ALL OF THIS?! HAVE YOU BEEN SPYING ON ME?

SPYING? APPARENTLY, YOU'VE BEEN SPYING ON US!

YEAH!

OKAY. ALL RIGHT. YOU'RE MOSTLY RIGHT.

TELL ME WHAT I MISSED.

I HAVE TO GO BACK A LITTLE...

I LIVE WITH MY MOMS:

RUTA (I CALL HER IMA)

AND OLIVIA (I CALL HER MOM)

SEE, YOU WERE RIGHT: I HAD CANCER TWO YEARS AGO (WHICH YOU CREEPILY KNOW SOMEHOW).

WE HAVE THE RESULTS OF OUR TESTING...

I DIDN'T UNDERSTAND ANYTHING THE DOCTOR SAID THEN...

HODGKIN'S LYMPHOMA...

...ONCOLOGIST...

...CHEMOTHERAPY...

BUT I FOUND OUT **PLENTY** SOON ENOUGH.

HODGKIN'S LYMPHOMA: A CANCER KIDS GET SOMETIMES.

Sick**Kids** Hospital

ONCOLOGIST: CANCER DOCTOR.

CHEMOTHERAPY ("CHEMO"): CANCER MEDICINE WITH SIDE EFFECTS LIKE LOSING YOUR HAIR AND BEING SO TIRED AND FEELING LIKE YOU HAVE TO BARF ALL THE TIME.

IT **IS** SERIOUS. SOME PEOPLE DIE FROM IT.

BUT **LOTS** GET BETTER.

AFTER A LONG, BAD TIME

I STARTED TO GET BETTER TOO.

181

CANCER MADE MY PARENTS EVEN MORE OVERPROTECTIVE.

DID YOU WASH YOUR HANDS?

YOU ARE NOT SHARING FOOD WITH OTHER KIDS.

NO, YOU CAN'T PLAY AT THEIR HOUSE!

I KNOW IT KEPT ME SAFE, BUT IT MADE ME BANANAS!

AND THIS SUMMER, EVEN THOUGH THE DOCTOR SAYS IT'S OKAY, THEY'RE BOTH STILL BONKERS:

THE POOL'S TOO GERMY!

THE SUN WILL BURN YOU!

THE OUTSIDE IS FULL OF INFECTIOUS DISEASES AND THE PLAGUE OR WHATEVER!

I'M SICK OF IT!

182

IMA THOUGHT THAT STUPID KINDERGARTEN FROG SPRINKLER OUT FRONT COULD REPLACE GOING TO A REAL POOL!

YOU CAN SPLASH RIGHT HERE IN THE YARD!

DON'T FORGET YOUR SUNSCREEN.

ISN'T THAT FUN?

REAPPLY EVERY HALF HOUR.

JUST BE CAREFUL...

AND KEEP YOUR HAT ON.

THE SUN IS HOTTEST BETWEEN NOON AND TWO PM.

ONLY GO OUT FOR SHORT BURSTS.

ACTUALLY, YOU LIKELY STILL HAVE SKIN SENSITIVITY AND COULD GET THIRD-DEGREE BURNS IN A SHORT TIME, UNPROTECTED.

YOU THINK I DON'T KNOW THAT?!

I DON'T TAKE THE GARBAGE OUT AT NIGHT WITHOUT SPF 100 ON!

YOU DON'T KNOW WHAT IT'S LIKE.

I'M CAREFUL!

I JUST NEED TO FEEL NORMAL.

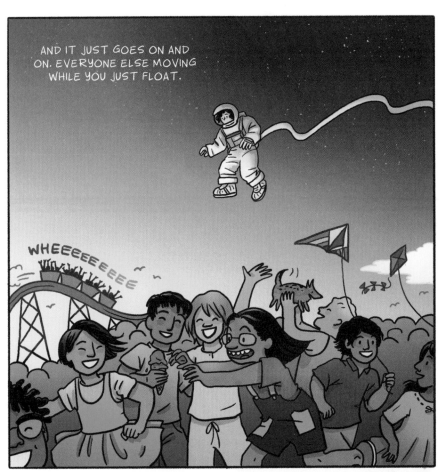

AND IT JUST GOES ON AND ON. EVERYONE ELSE MOVING WHILE YOU JUST FLOAT.

WHEEEEEEEEE

YOU DON'T KNOW HOW GOOD YOU GOT IT.

I HAD TO SIT INSIDE AND WATCH YOU TWO WALK PAST MY HOUSE EVERY DAY ON THE WAY TO THE POOL. I HATED YOU.

WELL, I DO LIKE IT!

WELL, ME TOO, BUT THAT'S NOT THE POINT.

THE POINT IS THAT OUR DAD WORKS **NIGHTS.**

AND SLEEPS DAYS!

AND OUR MOM'S AN ER DOCTOR.

...I'M ON THE FIVE A.M. TO FIVE P.M. NOW. CAN YOU COME BY THEN? NO?

FINDING BABYSITTERS IS HARD.

BUT I'M ELEVEN NOW AND OUR PARENTS AGREED WE COULD GO TO THE POOL—

BY OURSELVES!

BUT I'M IN CHARGE.

I'M SECOND IN CHARGE!

THERE'S NO SUCH THING. BESIDES, I'M IN CHARGE OF **YOU.**

ONLY IN AN EMERGENCY!

ALL THE TIME.

JUST EMERGENCIES.

YOU COULD HAVE REALLY HURT ENOCH. KILLED HIM EVEN.

YOU TRIED TO RUIN OUR SUMMER **ON PURPOSE.** IS THAT FAIR?

I DIDN'T MEAN TO! I JUST WANTED WHAT YOU HAD!

IT GOT REAL EXCITING SNEAKING AROUND. INSTEAD OF BEING BORED BY MYSELF ALL THE TIME.

I'D PACK A SNACK AND A BOOK OR SOME COMICS AND HANG OUT UNDER A TREE READING.

EVEN REGULAR APPLES TASTED BETTER BECAUSE NO ONE KNEW I WAS OUTSIDE, ALONE, EATING THEM.

I WORE THE HAT AND LONG SLEEVES AS A DISGUISE IN CASE ANY OF MY NEIGHBORS SAW ME.

WHO IS SHE? COULD BE ANYONE!

...ALSO TO PROTECT FROM THE SUN. CANCER SUCKS. FOR REAL.

BUT THE FUN WORE OFF. AFTER A WHILE, I WAS JUST SITTING OUTSIDE BY MYSELF.

I STARTED TO HATE LOOKING AT THE PEOPLE IN THE POOL.

I GUESS I COULD HAVE SNUCK INTO THE POOL TOO, BUT THAT CHLORINE SMELL IS HARD TO HIDE.

TOO TRUE.

AND WHAT IF MY MOM IS RIGHT ABOUT GERMS? WHAT IF I GOT SICK AGAIN?

bite bite...

SNIFF

THEN THIS ONE DAY A BALL ROLLED THROUGH THE FENCE.

I THREW IT BACK IN.

THERE IT IS!

NO ONE NOTICED ME.

IT'S LIKE THEY COULDN'T EVEN SEE ME.

LIKE ANYTHING OUTSIDE OF THE POOL DIDN'T MATTER.

LIKE I WAS INVISIBLE.

I STARTED TO TEST IT.

I TOOK SMALL THINGS.

OLIVER AND VEE BROUGHT SO MUCH STUFF...

THEY NEVER SAW ME.

THEY GOT TO BE INSIDE. I GOT THEIR STUFF.

WHERE'S MY DINOSAUR?

I DIDN'T TOUCH IT.

IT WAS **JUST** HERE!

IF MORE STUFF GOES MISSING, MOM AND DAD WON'T LET US COME TO THE POOL ANYMORE!

I'LL HELP YOU LOOK.

THIS ONE DAY I FOUND A SPOT ON THE FENCE WHERE THE LINKS WERE BROKEN.

I COULD FIT BIGGER THINGS THROUGH ...

I HAD TO WAIT A FEW DAYS BEFORE EVERYTHING LINED UP. AND THEN—THE OTHER DAY—OLIVER AND VEE SAT RIGHT NEXT TO THE HOLE **AND** HAD A BACKPACK WITH THEM THAT THEY SEEMED TO BE GIVING ALL THIS WEIRD ATTENTION.

HE'S STILL SLEEPING.

HE LOOKS HOT.

HE LIKES IT HOT. HIS TANK IS THIS HOT ALL THE TIME.

I KNOW.

WE GOTTA WATCH HIM LIKE CRAZY.

TOTALLY.

IF WE GET CAUGHT—

OR HE GOES MISSING—

YEAH.

IT WAS MY MOMENT.

BUT AS PROMISED, THEY WERE WATCHING PRETTY CLOSELY.

I NEEDED A DISTRACTION.

SOMEONE NEEDS A DIAPER CHANGE!

WHOA!

IT'S REAL!

EWW!

GROSS!

IT'S FAKE!

I BETTER GET OUT OF HERE...

I GUESS YOU KNOW WHAT HAPPENED AFTER THAT.

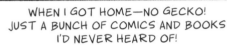

WHEN I GOT HOME—NO GECKO! JUST A BUNCH OF COMICS AND BOOKS I'D NEVER HEARD OF!

AND I ALMOST GOT CAUGHT! KUMI DIDN'T JUST RUN INTO ME—SHE TALKED TO ME!

IT WAS LIKE MY SUPERPOWER WAS GONE. I WASN'T INVISIBLE ANYMORE.

ARE YOU O—

I'VE STAYED AWAY FROM THE POOL SINCE THEN. I WAS AFRAID OF GETTING CAUGHT.

PLUS I HAD ALL THIS NEW STUFF TO READ.

MY STUFF...

BUT YOU GOT CAUGHT ANYWAY! AND BROUGHT TO JUSTICE!

YOU SAID YOU DIDN'T MEAN TO RUIN OUR SUMMER— IT SURE SOUNDS LIKE YOU **DID** MEAN TO.

YOU DID ALL THAT STUFF ON PURPOSE.

YEAH!

IT JUST HAPPENED! LIKE AN ACCIDENT!

THAT YOU PLANNED?!

I GET THAT YOUR SUMMER WASN'T WHAT YOU WANTED... AND THAT YOUR MOM WASN'T LISTENING.

...AND I ACTUALLY GET IT THAT MAYBE YOU LIED ABOUT IT A LITTLE.

TRUST ME, I GET IT.

BUT IT'S NOT FAIR TO RUIN SOMEONE ELSE'S SUMMER BECAUSE OF THAT! IF YOU'RE GONNA SNEAK AROUND...

...AT LEAST TRY TO HELP OTHER PEOPLE WHILE YOU'RE AT IT.

I ALWAYS WANTED ONE—OR A CHAMELEON MAYBE.

BUT AS ALWAYS: GERMS.

THEY'RE NOT GERMY! THEY'RE REPTILES! YOU COULDN'T EVEN GET SICK FROM ONE, I BET!

ACTUALLY, YOU CAN.

REPTILES CARRY DISEASE.

WHAT?

EW!

CAN'T AVOID HUMANS, THOUGH.

WE JUST USE MORE HAND SANITIZER.

SO DO HUMANS!

BUT FOR CHEMO KIDS, NO REPTILES.

SPEAKING TO KUMI CONFIRMED MY SUSPICIONS:
1. THERE WERE **TWO** BACKPACKS
2. THERE WAS ANOTHER PERSON INVOLVED. AND THANKS TO KUMI WE HAD A DESCRIPTION AND TWO MORE PIECES OF EVIDENCE.

KUMI'S DESCRIPTION:

"SHE HAD DARK, CURLY HAIR CHIN-LENGTH"

"BAGGY CLOTHES THAT COVERED A LOT OF SKIN"

"SHE WAS SMALL— MAYBE SEVEN OR EIGHT YEARS OLD OR OLDER AND JUST SMALL FOR HER AGE"

TWO PIECES OF EVIDENCE:

THE HAT.

THE BOOK.

FIRSTLY, A CLOSER INSPECTION OF THE HAT TURNED UP A FEW THINGS:

ONE: ON THE UNDERSIDE OF THE TAG—INITIALS.

A.M.

TWO: AN EVEN CLOSER INSPECTION SHOWED SOME OF THE MOST REVEALING EVIDENCE A DETECTIVE CAN HOPE FOR.

HAIR!

205

THE HAIR TOLD ME SOMETHING IMPORTANT ABOUT THE HAT'S OWNER.

IS IT SOMETHING GROSS? LIKE THEY HAVE LICE?

HEY!

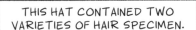

THIS HAT CONTAINED TWO VARIETIES OF HAIR SPECIMEN.

A FEW DARK, CURLY HAIRS OF MEDIUM LENGTH. CONSISTENT WITH KUMI'S DESCRIPTION OF THE GIRL SHE RAN INTO.

WE CAN DEDUCE THIS HAIR IS RECENT.

WHEN I LOOKED CLOSER, CAUGHT IN THE HAT LINER WAS REALLY SHORT HAIR.

JUST A FEW STRANDS...

BUT THEY WEREN'T CLIPPINGS: THESE HAIRS HAD FOLLICLES!

EW!

IT'S NOT GROSS. A FOLLICLE IS JUST A HAIR ROOT. ALL HAIR HAS THEM.

THESE HAIRS HAD BEEN CUT VERY SHORT FIRST ... AND THEN FALLEN OUT.

I DON'T SEE A LOT OF KIDS WITH BUZZCUTS AND HAIR LOSS ...

CELEBS VISIT KIDS' CANCER WARD.

...UNLESS THEY HAVE CANCER.

FOR A KID TO USE THE SAME HAT FROM HAIR LOSS TO CHIN-LENGTH HAIR AND NOT OUTGROW IT ... CHANCES ARE SHE'S SMALL FOR HER AGE.

THE INITIALS SUGGEST A PROTECTIVE PARENT. WHICH OFTEN MEANS AN EXTRA SNEAKY KID.

A.M.

SURVIVOR

• SMALL

• SNEAKY

I KNEW OUR CULPRIT HAD THE INITIALS "A.M.," WAS A CANCER SURVIVOR, AND ALTHOUGH SHE LOOKS SMALL, SHE IS CRAFTY, AND SHOULD NOT BE UNDERESTIMATED.

I MOVED ON TO THE BOOK.

HERE'S WHAT I FOUND:

NOT A LIBRARY BOOK.

NO NAME OR INITIALS ANYWHERE.

NO WRITING INSIDE.

THIS BOOK IS USUALLY COVERED IN GRADE EIGHT! ...

CONFIRMATION: OUR CULPRIT WAS SMALL AND CLEVER.

THEN THE BREAKTHROUGH: A BOOKMARK!

BETTER THAN A REAL BOOKMARK, THIS WAS A CHUNK OF PAPER, RIPPED FROM WHATEVER WAS LYING AROUND.

VOILA!

RED DOG SECURITY
151 DUNDAS WEST  TORONTO, ON.
NOTICE OF UPDATE TO SERVICE
MALINOWSKI
BORDEN S...

I HAD A LAST NAME AND A STREET NAME.

NOW IT WAS TIME FOR FIELDWORK.

THE NEXT DAY...

I'M LEAVING!

WITH JAMILA?

YES, MOTHER.

I HIT THE STREETS.

SO YOU WERE JUST GOING TO WALK UP AND DOWN BORDEN STREET AND HOPE YOU SEE A GIRL ON THE LAWN? BORDEN'S A LONG STREET!

IT SURE IS.

WELL...I MADE SOME ERRORS IN JUDGMENT THERE AND WAS ALMOST FORCED TO GIVE UP.

BUT I HAD A STROKE OF LUCK.

I'M LEAVING.

WHY CAN'T YOU JUST TELL ME WHAT'S GOING ON?!

WHY ARE YOU SMILING?

I WAS SMILING BECAUSE THE CASE WAS SOLVED.

208

THE EVIDENCE, PLUS A LITTLE PUNCH-IN-THE-GUT FEELING THAT I'VE COME TO TRUST...IT ALL SAID THIS WAS THE PLACE.

A. MALINOWSKI LIVES HERE. AND HERE YOU ARE.

BUT HOW DID YOU KNOW MY NAME WAS ANGIE?

YOUR MOM SAID IT AFTER YOU ANSWERED THE DOOR.

OH, YEAH. DANG.

WHEN YOU EXPLAIN IT, IT ALL SEEMS SO OBVIOUS.

209

I...I GOTTA RUN INSIDE FOR A SECOND.

YOU KNOW...

IT'S ACTUALLY REALLY IMPRESSIVE—

THANK YOU, BUT THE WORK IS ITS OWN REWAR—

NO, HOW ANGIE PLANNED THIS WHOLE THING OUT.

YES.

ANGIE.

PLANNING A DIVERSION,

BEING KEPT IN ALL SUMMER...

SHE HAD A VERY METHODICAL APPROACH.

METHODICAL?

METHOD-BASED...IT WAS WELL-PLANNED. AS KUMI SAID.

HEY.

IMAGINE IF I HAD TO WATCH SHIRLEY PASS MY HOUSE EVERY DAY AND COULDN'T GO ALONG...

YOU'RE RIGHT.

THANK YOU.

IT'S NOT OKAY... BUT I THINK SHE PICKED ON YOU BOTH FOR A REASON.

OH YEAH?

SHE SAID SHE SAW YOU EVERY DAY AND WANTED MORE THAN ANYTHING TO GO **WITH** YOU.

IT GOT ALL ROTTEN WHEN HER PARENTS WOULDN'T LET HER OUT.

BUT I THINK SHE REALLY WANTS TO BE FRIENDS.

MAYBE SHE THOUGHT IF YOU GOT KICKED OUT OF THE POOL, YOU'D WIND UP IN THE PARK TOO ... THEN SHE COULD PLAY WITH YOU INSTEAD OF WORKING AGAINST YOU.

THAT'S A TERRIBLE WAY TO MAKE FRIENDS!

HA-HA! YEAH!

NO, FOR SURE IT IS.

I THINK IT'S BEEN A WHILE SINCE SHE HAD ANY.

I GUESS I NEVER THOUGHT OF—

HERE SHE COMES!

I ...

I HAVE ALL OF YOUR STUFF.

213

YOU'VE ONLY HAD THIS FOR A FEW DAYS AND YOU READ THIS FAR?

I READ A LOT. I FINISHED ALL THE OTHERS.

WHOA.

DRAGON

HAVE YOU READ THESE?

IS THAT A COMIC?

YEAH, THEY'RE COOL. I'M TRYING TO DRAW THIS DRAGON, BUT IT'S HARD.

THAT LOOKS AWESOME.

DID YOU READ THESE?

MY MOM'S ANNOYED WITH DRAGON BOOKS, BUT—

THEY'RE SO GREAT!

JINX!

DRAGONS DROOL, DINOSAURS RULE!

215

# Chapter 15

A FEW DAYS LATER

YES!

NOW TRY IT AGAIN!

OOF!

SWISH

HA-HA, YES!

SHIRLEY, YOU'RE SO GOOD AT THIS!

I SHOULD COACH YOU AND WE COULD PLAY ONE-ON-ONE.

WE COULD PLAY TWO-ON-TWO IF OTHER KIDS SHOW UP. MAYBE MY BROTHER'D COME BY AFTER HIS CAMP AND GIVE US POINTERS ON—

—SHOOTING.

IS IT A CASE?

BETTER.

VEE AND OLIVER GOT BACK IN THE POOL!

REALLY?!

VEE SAID SHE JUST TALKED TO GREGSON INSTEAD OF LESTRAD.

THAT JERK.

NO
DIVING

SUCH A JERK. GREGSON SAID KIDS FIGHT ALL THE TIME AND THEY NEVER SHOULD HAVE BEEN BANNED IN THE FIRST PLACE.

NOW VEE AND OLIVER ARE PLANNING A REVENGE PRANK AGAINST LESTRAD.

THEY'RE GOING TO GET BANNED FOR REAL.

ANGIE CAN GO WITH THEM ONCE A WEEK.

FOR TWO HOURS.

STARTING AFTER TWO PM WHEN THE UV INDEX DROPS.

ANGIE'S MOM AND MINE SHOULD BE FRIENDS.

A DANGEROUS COMBINATION.

HEY SHIRLEY.

YES?

HOW COME YOU BROUGHT KUMI AND VEE AND OLIVER ALONG WHEN WE WENT TO CONFRONT ANGIE?

219

WELL...

I KNEW ANGIE DID IT. AND I HAD A GOOD IDEA WHY—BUT KUMI AND VEE AND OLIVER DIDN'T.

I THOUGHT IT WAS BETTER THAT THEY HEAR ANGIE EXPLAIN HERSELF IN PERSON.

WHEN SOMEBODY TELLS THEIR OWN STORY, IT'S EASIER TO JUDGE THEIR MOTIVATIONS...

AND DECIDE ON A FAIR RESPONSE.

YEAH, I GUESS IT WAS BETTER.

AND I THOUGHT ANGIE WOULD LIKE TO MAKE SOME FRIENDS.

CASE CLOSED

ACKNOWLEDGMENT AND ONGOING THANKS
TO THE PEOPLE WHO SUPPORTED THIS BOOK
IN SO MANY WAYS:

Mariko Tamaki, whose support and collaboration cleared this path; my agent, Anjali Singh, who helped shape this book in its earliest days & championed it onward, as well as Ayesha Pande and everyone at Ayesha Pande Literary; my patient and generous editor Dana Chidiac, designer Jenny Kelly, early editor & keen eye Namrata Tripathi, and everyone at Dial Books for Young Readers and Penguin Random House; Samra Habib, Ryan North, Aisha Jamal, Sameer Farooq, Sadiya Ansari, Sydney Smith, Jane Edmundson, Sel Ghebrihewot, Sana A. Malik, Teela Wyman, and Brooke Day, who read drafts, provided inspiration and context, and answered questions over the long course of several years; Kat Verhoeven, whose flatting skills saved my life, and for her contributions to page 169 in particular; Sam Maggs, Hope Nicholson, every one of my studiomates, Dustin McMurphy, Jaime Graves, David Ross, and Mikey Bennington; Alana and the whole Trumpy family for giving an only child a chance to see how a big family lives. Special thanks to Leigh Stein, Lux Alptraum, and the Binders. And to my mom, Lottie, who is included in the dedication.